UKRAINIAN FOLK TALES

TALES ABOUT ANIMALS

DRAWINGS BY Y. RACHOV

Fredonia Books
Amsterdam, The Netherlands

Ukrainian Folk Tales:
Tales About Animals

ISBN: 1-4101-0706-X

Fredonia Books
Amsterdam, The Netherlands
http://www.fredoniabooks.com

CONTENTS

THE OLD MAN'S MITTEN

An Old Man was walking through the forest one day with his Dog. He walked and he walked and he dropped his mitten.

Just then a Mouse came scuttling up and when he saw the mitten he stopped and climbed right in and said:

"This is where I'm going to live."

After a while a Frog came hopping up and when he saw the mitten he stopped and called out:

"Croak! Croak! Who is living in this mitten?"

5

"I am. Crunch-Munch the Mouse. And who are you?"

"I'm Hop-Stop the Frog. Let me in!"

"All right. Jump in!"

So the Frog jumped in and the Mouse moved over and the two of them made their home in the mitten.

After a while a Rabbit came scurrying up and when he saw the mitten he stopped and called out:

"Hello there! Who is living in this mitten?"

"We are. Crunch-Munch the Mouse and Hop-Stop the Frog. And who are you?"

"I'm Fleet-Feet the Rabbit. May I join you?"

"All right. Jump in!"

So the Rabbit jumped in and the Mouse and the Frog moved over and the three of them made their home in the mitten.

After a while a Fox came scampering up.

"You-hoo! Who is living in this mitten?"

"We are. Crunch-Munch the Mouse, Hop-Stop the Frog and Fleet-Feet the Rabbit. And who are you?"

"I'm Smily-Wily the Fox. Won't you make room for me?"

So the Mouse and the Frog and the Rabbit moved over and the Fox climbed in and the four of them made their home in the mitten.

After a while a Wolf came stalking up and when he saw the mitten he stopped and called out:

"Hello, friends! Who is living in this mitten?"

"We are. Crunch-Munch the Mouse, Hop-Stop the Frog, Fleet-Feet the Rabbit and Smily-Wily the Fox. And who are you?"

"I'm Howly-Prowly the Wolf. And I mean to get in!"

"Very well. Go ahead!"

So the Wolf climbed in and the Mouse and the Frog and the Rabbit and the Fox moved over and the five of them made their home in the mitten.

After a while a wild Boar came sauntering up.

"Grunt! Grunt! Who is living in this mitten?"

"We are. Crunch-Munch the Mouse, Hop-Stop the Frog, Fleet-Feet the Rabbit, Smily-Wily the Fox and Howly-Prowly the Wolf. And who are you?"

"I'm Snout-Rout the Boar. And I'm sure you want me, too."

"Dear, dear! Everybody wants to get into this mitten. You won't find it easy to get in, Snout-Rout!"

"Never mind! I'll manage!"

"In you go, then! But don't say we didn't warn you!"

So the Boar squeezed in and then there were six of them in the mitten and they were so cramped that they couldn't move!

By and by with a crackling of twigs a bear came lumbering up and when he saw the mitten he stopped and bellowed:

"Hello, good people! Who is living in this mitten?"

"We are. Crunch-Munch the Mouse, Hop-Stop the Frog, Fleet-Feet the Rabbit, Smily-Wily the Fox, Howly-Prowly the Wolf and Snout-Rout the Boar. And who are you?"

"Ho-ho-ho! I'm Grumbly-Rumbly the Bear. And though you're quite a crowd, I know you'll make room for me!"

"How can we? We're cramped as it is!"

"Where there's a will, there's a way!"

"Oh, all right, edge in, but don't forget that you're not the only one."

So the Bear squeezed in, too, and now there were seven of them inside and they were so cramped that the mitten was fit to burst.

It was just about then that the Old Man missed his mitten and decided to go back in search of it. He walked and he walked and his Dog ran and ran until at last he saw the mitten lying in the snow and moving!

"Bow-wow-wow!" went the Dog.

And the seven friends inside the mitten were so frightened that out they jumped and away they ran as fast as their legs could carry them.

Then the Old Man came up and he picked up his mitten and that was the end of that.

THE LITTLE STRAW BULL
WITH THE TARRED BACK

Once upon a time there lived an Old Man and an
Old Woman. The Old Man made tar and the Old Woman
kept house.

Now the Old Woman began to fret and to worry and
she said to the Old Man:

"Do make me a little bull of straw."

10

"What's come over you, you silly Old Woman, what do you want with a bull?"

"I shall take him out to graze!"

There was nothing to be done, so the Old Man made a little bull of straw and he smeared his back and sides over with tar. And in the morning the Old Woman led the Little Straw Bull out to pasture and she took her spinning with her.

She sat down on a hill-side and she spun her cloth and said:

"Graze, graze, Little Bull—Little Tarred Back!
Graze, graze, Little Bull—Little Tarred Back!"

And she spun and she spun till at last she dozed away.

All of a sudden out of the great dark forest a Bear came running.

He lumbered straight up to the Little Bull and said: "Who are you?"

"I am the Little Straw Bull with the Tarred Back," said the Little Bull.

"Give me some tar, Little Bull, for the dogs have torn my side."

But the Little Straw Bull just stood there and said not another word.

The Bear flew into a temper and he clawed at the Little Bull's side and lo! he was stuck fast!

Now the Old Woman woke up and she cried at the top of her voice:

"Make haste and come here, Old Man! The Little Bull has caught a Bear!"

And the Old Man came running and he seized the Bear and threw him into the cellar.

On the next day the Old Woman led the Little Bull out to pasture again and she took her spinning with her. She sat down on a hill-side and she spun her cloth and said:

"Graze, graze, Little Bull—Little Tarred Back!
Graze, graze, Little Bull—Little Tarred Back!"

And she spun and she spun till at last she dozed away.

All of a sudden out of the great dark forest a Wolf came running.

He saw the Little Bull and said:

"Who are you?"

"I am the Little Straw Bull with the Tarred Back," the Little Bull replied.

"Give me some tar, for the dogs have torn my side!"

"Take it."

But no sooner did the Wolf touch the Little Bull than he was stuck fast!

The old Woman woke up and she cried:

"Old Man, Old Man, the Little Bull has caught a Wolf!"

The Old Man came running and he seized the Wolf and threw him into the cellar.

On the third day the Old Woman took the Little Bull out to pasture again and she sat there and spun her cloth. She spun and she spun till at last she dozed away.

By and by a Fox came running up and she said to the Little Bull:

"Who are you?"

"I am the Little Straw Bull with the Tarred Back."

"Give me some tar, dear Little Bull, for the dogs have torn my side!"

"Take it."

And so the Fox, too, was stuck fast to the Little Bull's back. The Old Woman woke up and she called to the Old Man. And the Old Man threw the Fox into the cellar.

So now there were three of them in the cellar.

The Old Man sat down on the trap-door and he began to sharpen his knife. Said the Old Man:

"I think I shall skin the Bear and make myself a fine coat."

The Bear heard him and was very frightened.

"Do not kill me, Old Man!" he cried. "Let me go free and I shall bring you some honey."

"You aren't going to fool me, are you?"

"Oh, no."

"Well, see that you don't."

And he set the Bear free and himself began to sharpen his knife again.

And the Wolf heard him and said:

"Why do you sharpen your knife, Old Man?"

"I am going to skin you and make myself a warm hat for the winter."

"Let me go free, and I shall bring you a herd of sheep."

"Well, see that you don't fool me."

And with that he let the Wolf go free and himself began to sharpen his knife again.

"Good Old Man, tell me, why do you sharpen your knife?" asked the Fox.

"You have fine fluffy fur," the Old Man replied. "It will make a nice collar for my Old Woman's coat."

"Please do not kill me, Old Man! I shall bring you some chickens and ducks and geese."

"Well, see that you don't fool me."

And with that he let the Fox go free.

In the morning, before dawn had set in or day had broken, there came a rap-tap-tap at the door.

"Someone is knocking, Old Man!" the Old Woman cried. "Go and see who it is."

The Old Man opened the door, and there stood the Bear with a whole hive of honey!

The Old Man took the honey and put it away when suddenly there came a rap-tap-tap at the door again.

This time it was the Wolf with a whole herd of sheep. And very soon after the Fox appeared, bringing the chickens, the geese and the ducks.

The Old Man and the Old Woman were overjoyed. From that day on they lived in good health and cheer and grew richer from year to year.

SIR CAT-O-PUSS

Once upon a time there lived a Man who had a Cat so old that he could not even catch mice.

"What do I want with this old Cat of mine?" said the Man to himself. "I think I'll go to the forest and leave him there."

And that was just what he did.

The Cat sat under a fir-tree and wept when lo! Smily-Wily the Fox came running up.

"Who are you?" she called.

The Cat puffed himself out and said:

"P-r-r, f-r-r! I am Sir Cat-o-Puss."

Smily-Wily the Fox was very pleased to make the acquaintance of so great a personage and said:

"Why don't you marry me, Sir Cat-o-Puss? I shall be a good wife to you and feed you well."

"Very well," replied Sir Cat-o-Puss, "I don't mind."

And so the Cat and the Fox were married and they set up house in Smily-Wily's hut.

Now Smily-Wily tried very hard to be nice to Sir Cat-o-Puss. She would catch him a chicken or bring him some little wood animal for supper. She herself might go without, but she was sure to bring him anything he wanted.

One day Fleet-Feet the Rabbit met Smily-Wily the Fox and said to her:

"I am going to come and woo you, Smily-Wily."

"No, Fleet-Feet, you mustn't," replied Smily-Wily. "I have Sir Cat-o-Puss living in my house now. He might claw you to pieces."

And Sir Cat-o-Puss came out of the hut, arched his back, puffed himself out and said:

"P-r-r, f-r-r!"

And Fleet-Feet the Rabbit nearly died of fright when he heard him. Off he ran to the forest and he told the Wolf, the Bear and the Wild Boar that he had just seen a terrible beast by the name of Sir Cat-o-Puss.

Now the four of them wanted to be on good terms with Sir Cat-o-Puss and, with this in mind, they decided to have him and Smily-Wily the Fox to dinner. They began to talk over the dishes, and the Wolf said:

"I shall go and get the meat and bacon for the borshch."

"And I shall go and fetch the beets and potatoes," said the Boar.

"And I shall bring the honey for dessert," said the Bear.

And as for Fleet-Feet the Rabbit, he ran off to get some cabbage.

They cooked the dinner and set the table, but they couldn't agree as to which of them was to go and fetch Sir Cat-o-Puss and Smily-Wily the Fox.

"I am fat and will soon be out of breath," said the Bear.

"I am clumsy and will take too long about it," said the Boar.

"I am old and don't hear so well," said the Wolf.

So Fleet-Feet the Rabbit was the one to go.

He ran up to Smily-Wily's hut and he knocked at the window three times—knock-knock-knock!

Out jumped Smily-Wily, and there was Fleet-Feet standing before her on his hind paws.

"What do you want?" she asked.

"The Wolf, the Bear, the Boar and I would like to have you, Smily-Wily, and Sir Cat-o-Puss to dinner to-day," Fleet-Feet replied and off he ran.

He came to where the three friends were waiting, and the Bear said:

"I hope you haven't forgotten to tell them to bring their spoons?"

"Oh, dear, so I have!" cried Fleet-Feet and he set off at a run again for Smily-Wily's hut.

He knocked at the window and said:

"Don't forget to bring your spoons with you when you come!"

And Smily-Wily replied:

"Don't worry, we won't!"

Then Smily-Wily put on her best apparel, took Sir Cat-o-Puss's arm and off they started.

And Sir Cat-o-Puss puffed himself out again and he let out his "p-r-r, f-r-r!" and his eyes glowed like two green candles.

At this the Wolf was very frightened and he crouched down under a bush. The Boar crawled under the table, the Bear climbed as best he could up a tree and Fleet-Feet the Rabbit hid in his rabbit-hole.

When Sir Cat-o-Puss saw the meat on the table, he rushed toward it, crying, "Miaow, miaow, miaow!" and began to gobble it up very fast indeed.

And the four animals thought that he was crying, "More, more, more!" and said in a whisper:

"What a glutton! Nothing's too much for him!"

Sir Cat-o-Puss had his fill of the food and the drink, curled up on the table and fell asleep.

And the Boar, who was hiding under the table, now moved his tail slightly.

Sir Cat-o-Puss thought it was a mouse and rushed under the table. When he saw the Boar, he was terribly frightened and jumped up on the tree where the Bear was sitting.

The Bear thought that Sir Cat-o-Puss wanted to fight him and climbed up higher. But the branches broke under him and he tumbled down, straight on the bush behind which the Wolf was crouching.

The Wolf thought that his end had come and took to his heels! And so fast did he and the Bear run that even Fleet-Feet the Rabbit could not catch up with them.

And Sir Cat-o-Puss climbed up on the table and began to gobble up the bacon and honey. He and Smily-Wily ate up all there was and then they went home.

As for the Bear, the Boar, the Wolf and the Rabbit, they came together again after a while and said:

"What a terrible beast Sir Cat-o-Puss is! He is so small and he nearly ate up all the four of us!"

THE CAT AND THE COCK

Once upon a time there lived a Cat and a Cock. They loved each other dearly and always lived together, in one little hut. One day the Cat prepared to go to the forest for wood and he said to the Cock:

"I am off to the forest to get some wood, Petenka, and you must sit on the stove and eat your kalaches. Let no one into the hut and don't go out, no matter who calls you."

"Very well, very well," the Cock replied, and he shut the door tight behind the Cat.

Now a Fox came running up, and you all know how she loves fresh chicken, and she called to the Cock:

"Come, Petenka, Little Cock,
Turn the key in yonder lock!
I shall give you grains of wheat,
Large as large and sweet as sweet.
If you don't, then, I swear by my kith and kin
Through the window I'll climb in!"

And the Cock called back in reply:

"Cock-a-doodle-do, cock-a-doodle-do,
As I promised Puss, thus will I do!"

The Fox broke the window, seized the Cock by the head with her teeth and carried him off. And the Cock called out to the Cat ever so sorrowfully:

"Save me, Brother Puss, I pray!
Foxy's taking me far away,
Beyond the dark forests
And the blue-green dales,
Beyond the swift rivers
And the distant vales,
Beyond the hills
And the mountains high—
O, save me, Puss, before I die!"

The Cat heard the Cock and he came running. He snatched the Cock away from the Fox, brought him home and said again:

"You mustn't answer her, when the Fox comes, whatever you do. I am going a long way off this time."
And off he went.

22

As soon as the Fox saw the Cat leave, she came running again.

She ran to the window and knocked and called in a voice that was ever so sweet:

"Come, Petenka, Little Cock,
Turn the key in yonder lock!
I shall give you grains of wheat,
Large as large and sweet as sweet.
If you don't, then, I swear by my kith and kin,
Through the window I'll climb in!"

And the Cock couldn't keep from answering her and called:

"Cock-a-doodle-do, cock-a-doodle-do,
As I promised Puss, thus will I do!"

Then the Fox burst into the hut, gobbled up the borshch and the porridge, seized the Cock by the head with her teeth and carried him off. And the Cock called out:

"Save me, Brother Puss, I pray!
Foxy's taking me far away,
Beyond the dark forests
And the blue-green dales,
Beyond the swift rivers
And the distant vales,
Beyond the hills
And the mountains high,
O, save me, Puss, before I die!"

He called once and no one came, and he called a second time and the Cat came running. He snatched the Cock away from the Fox, brought him home and said to him very sternly indeed:

"You must sit on the stove, Petenka, and eat your kalaches, and when the Fox comes and calls to you,

24

you mustn't answer her! I shall go far, far away this time, and no matter how loud you call, I shan't hear you!"

The Cat went off, and there was the Fox, if you please, calling to the Cock:

"Come, Petenka, Little Cock,
Turn the key in yonder lock!
I shall give you grains of wheat,
Large as large and sweet as sweet.
If you don't, then, I swear by my kith and kin,
Through the window I'll climb in!"

And the Cock couldn't keep from answering her and he called back:

"Cock-a-doodle-do, cock-a-doodle-do,
As I promised Puss, thus will I do!"

Then the Fox jumped in through the window, gobbled up the borshch and the porridge, seized the Cock by the head with her teeth and carried him off.

The Cock called to the Cat once and he called to him a second time and a third.... But the Cat had gone a long way off and never heard him. And the Fox carried the Cock off to her house, for she thought the little foxes would like having him for dinner.

That evening the Cat came back from the forest, and lo! the Cock was gone. The Cat was very sad indeed and he thought and thought till he thought of a way of bringing the Cock back. He took a bandore and a hand-embroidered sack and went to the Fox's hut.

Now the Fox was out, for she had gone hunting, but she left her four daughters and her little son Filipók at home.

And the Cat went and stood under the window and he began to play on his bandore and to sing very sweetly indeed:

"Foxy's house is new and tall,
Her four young daughters are beauties all,
And little Filipók, her son,
Is ever full of joy and fun.
Come outside and hear me play
Tunes and carols, loud and gay!"

Now the Fox's eldest daughter felt that she must go out and see who it was playing and she said to her sisters:

"Stay here in the house and I shall go and see who it is that plays so well."

She came out of the house, and the Cat rapped her smartly on the nose—whack! whack! and then he whisked her into his sack!

And he began to sing again:

"Foxy's house is new and tall,
And her four young daughters are beauties all!"

Now the Fox's second daughter felt that she must go out and see who it was, and she ran out of the hut and the Cat rapped her on the nose—whack! whack! and he whisked her into his sack!

And then he began to play on his bandore again and to sing ever so sweetly:

"Foxy's house is new and tall,
And her four young daughters are beauties all!"

The Fox's third daughter now ran out of the hut, and the Cat gave her a whack on the nose, and the fourth came running out, and she fared like the rest. Then little Filipók tripped out, and the Cat popped him into the sack, too.

There sat the five little foxes in the hand-embroidered sack, with never a word.

The Cat tied the sack with a rope and he came inside the Fox's hut. And lo! there lay the Cock on the bench with hardly a breath of life left in him at all. His feathers were all plucked out of him and one of his legs was torn off. And there was a pot of water boiling in the stove in which he was to be cooked.

The Cat caught the Cock by the tail and said:

"Come, Petenka, little brother, wake up!"

And the Cock started up and was about to jump to his feet with a cock-a-doodle-do—but, no, how could he with one of his legs gone!

Then the Cat took the Cock's torn leg and he glued it on to its old place again and he stuck the Cock's feathers back in again, too. In a word, he fixed the Cock up as best he could.

Then the two of them ate up all there was in the Fox's hut, broke up all the pots and pans and went their way home.

And there they live to this day very quietly and munch their bread. And the Cock now does everything the Cat tells him to and never, never disobeys him. For suffering has taught him wisdom.

4*

THE WOLF,
THE DOG AND THE CAT

Once upon a time there lived a Peasant who had a Dog. While the Dog was young, he guarded his master's house, but when he grew old, his master chased him away. The Dog roamed through the steppe, caught mice and other little animals there and ate them.

One day the Dog saw a Wolf coming toward him.

"Hello, Dog!" the Wolf said.

The Dog made a polite reply, and the Wolf asked: "Where are you going, Dog?"

"While I was young," the Dog explained, "my master was quite fond of me, for I watched over his house. But when I grew old, he chased me away."

"You must be hungry, Dog," said the Wolf.

"I am. Very," replied the Dog.

"Well, then, come with me, and I shall feed you."

So off the Dog went with the Wolf. Now their way lay through the steppe, and by and by the Wolf saw a herd of sheep at pasture and said to the Dog:

"Go and see who those creatures are, grazing there."

The Dog went and looked and he soon came running back.

"Those are sheep," he said.

"A plague on them! If we try to eat them, we'll have our teeth full of wool and nothing but empty bellies to show for it. Let us go further, Dog!"

So on they went, and by and by the Wolf saw a flock of geese in the steppe.

"Go and see who those creatures are, browsing there," he said to the Dog.

The Dog went and looked and he soon came running back.

"Those are geese," he said.

"A plague on them! If we try to eat them, we'll have our teeth full of feathers and nothing but empty bellies to show for it. Let us go further!"

So on they went, and by and by the Wolf saw a horse at pasture.

"Go and see who that creature is, feeding there," he said.

The Dog went and looked and he soon came running back.

"That is a horse," he said.

"Well, we'll eat him," said the Wolf.

So they ran toward the horse, and the Wolf pawed at the ground and gnashed his teeth, all to make himself very angry.

Said he to the Dog:

"Tell me, Dog, is my tail quivering?"

And the Dog looked and said that indeed it was.

"And now," said the Wolf, "see if my eyes have grown bleary."

"Indeed they have," the Dog replied.

Then the Wolf sprang up and he seized the horse by the mane, dashed him to the ground and tore him to pieces. And he and the Dog began to feast on the horse's flesh. The Wolf was young and soon filled his belly, but the Dog was old and he gnawed and gnawed and still ate hardly anything. Other dogs ran up and they drove him away.

So the Dog set down the road again and, coming toward him, he saw a Cat as old as himself who was roaming the steppe in search of mice.

"Hello there, Brother Puss!" said the Dog. "Where are you going?"

"I am going wherever the road takes me. When I was young, I served my master by catching mice. But when I grew old and slow and my sight dimmed, my master stopped feeding me and he turned me out of the house. So now here I am knocking about the world."

Said the Dog:

"Well, then, come along, Brother Puss, and I shall feed you." For the Dog now decided to do just what the Wolf had done.

So the Dog and the Cat set off down the road together.

By and by the Dog saw a herd of sheep at pasture and he said to the Cat:

"Go and see who those creatures are, grazing there, Brother Puss."

The Cat went and looked and he soon came running back.

"Those are sheep," he said.

"A plague on them! We'll have our teeth full of wool and nothing but empty bellies to show for it. Let us go further!"

So on they went, and by and by the Dog saw a flock of geese in the steppe.

Said he to the Cat:

"Run and see who those creatures are, browsing there, Brother Puss!"

The Cat went and looked and he soon came running back.

"Those are geese," he said.

"A plague on them! We'll have our teeth full of feathers and nothing but empty bellies to show for it."

And so the two of them went their way further. They walked and they walked and by and by the Dog saw a horse at pasture.

Said the Dog:

"Run and see who that creature is, feeding there, Brother Puss."

The Cat went and looked and he soon came running back.

"That is a horse," he said.

"Well," said the Dog, "we'll kill him and then we'll have enough food and to spare."

So the Dog began to paw at the ground and to gnash his teeth, all to make himself very angry.

Said he to the Cat:

"See if my tail is quivering, Brother Puss."

"No," the Cat replied, "it isn't."

Then the Dog began to paw at the ground again to make himself very angry indeed.

Said he to the Cat:

"Isn't my tail quivering now, Brother Puss? Say that it is!"

The Cat looked and he said:

"Well, yes, it is, just a wee bit."

"Watch and see, we'll soon get the better of the horse!" said the Dog.

And he began to paw at the ground again.

"See if my eyes have grown bleary, Brother Puss," said he after a while.

"No, they haven't," the Cat replied.

"That's a lie! You must say that they have."

"Very well, they have grown bleary if you say so, I don't mind," said the Cat.

Then the Dog flew into a temper and he fell on the horse. But the horse kicked out with his hoofs and he struck the Dog in the head! And the Dog fell to the ground and his eyes popped out. And the Cat ran up to him and said:

"Ah, Little Brother, now your eyes have indeed grown bleary!"

NIBBLY-QUIBBLY THE GOAT

Once upon a time there lived an Old Man and an Old Woman. One day the Old Man went off to the fair and he bought a Goat. He brought the Goat home, went to bed and on the next day sent his eldest son to take the Goat out to graze. The youth pastured the Goat till evening and then he drove her home. He drove her straight to the gate, and there the Old Man his father stood in a pair of red boots. Said the Old Man:

"Little Goat, Little Nibbly-Quibbly, have you had enough to eat and drink?"

"No, Grandpa," the Goat replied, "I have not drunk nor eaten.

> As I ran by a tree with a hop and a skip,
> I whisked off a leaf and nibbled the tip.
> As I ran by a brook with a skip and a hop,
> I scooped up some water and had a drop!

And that was all that I ate and all that I drank."

The Old Man was very angry with his son and he turned him out of the house.

On the next day he sent his younger son to take the Goat out to graze. The youth pastured the Goat till evening and then he drove her home. He drove her straight to the gate, and there stood the Old Man his father in a pair of red boots. Said the Old Man:

"Little Goat, Little Nibbly-Quibbly, have you had enough to eat and drink?"

"No, Grandpa," replied the Goat, "I have not drunk nor eaten.

> As I ran by a tree with a hop and a skip,
> I whisked off a leaf and nibbled the tip.
> As I ran by a brook with a skip and a hop,
> I scooped up some water and had a drop!

And that was all that I ate and all that I drank."

So the Old Man turned his younger son out of the house, too. On the third day he sent the Old Woman to graze the Goat. The Old Woman led the Goat out to pasture and she pastured her all the day long and in the evening she drove her home. And there stood the Old Man by the gate in his red boots. Said the Old Man:

"Little Goat, Little Nibbly-Quibbly, have you had enough to eat and drink?"

"No, Grandpa, I have not drunk nor eaten.

As I ran by a tree with a hop and a skip,
I whisked off a leaf and nibbled the tip.
As I ran by a brook with a skip and a hop,
I scooped up some water and had a drop!

And that was all that I drank and all that I ate."

So the Old Man sent the Old Woman away, too.

On the fourth day he went himself to graze the Goat. He pastured her all the day long, and when evening came, he drove her out on to the road and himself ran ahead and stood by the gate of his house in his red boots.

Said the Old Man:

"Little Goat, Little Nibbly-Quibbly, have you had enough to eat and drink?"

"No, Grandpa, I have not drunk nor eaten.

As I ran by a tree with a hop and a skip,
I whisked off a leaf and nibbled the tip.
As I ran by a brook with a skip and a hop,
I scooped up some water and had a drop!

And that was all that I drank and all that I ate."

The Old Man was very angry. He went to a blacksmith's and had his knife sharpened, and he was about to cut the Goat's throat, but the Goat tore herself loose and ran off to the forest. She saw a rabbit's hut there, came inside and hid herself on the stove.

By and by the Rabbit ran in and he saw that there was someone in his hut. Said the Rabbit:

"Who, who is there in my hut?"
And the Goat sat there on the stove and said:

> "I am Nibbly-Quibbly the Goat,
> With a torn skin and coat,
> To the fair I was brought
> And for three groshes bought.
> I will frighten you off with a bleat,
> I will stamp-stamp on you with my feet,
> With my horns I will hook you and crush you,
> With my tail away I will brush you,
> And that will be the end of you!"

The Rabbit was very frightened and he ran out of the hut, sat down under a tree and began to cry. All of a sudden a Bear came lolloping up.

"Why are you crying, Bunny-Runny?" he asked.

"How can I help it, Grumbly-Rumbly, when a terrible beast is sitting in my hut!"

"I am going to chase him out!" said the Bear, and off he ran to the hut.

"Who, who is sitting in Bunny-Runny's hut?" he called.

And the Goat replied from the stove:

> "I am Nibbly-Quibbly the Goat,
> With a torn skin and coat,
> To the fair I was brought
> And for three groshes bought.
> I will frighten you off with a bleat,
> I will stamp-stamp on you with my feet,
> With my horns I will hook you and crush you,
> With my tail away I will brush you,
> And that will be the end of you!"

The Bear was very frightened and out he ran.

"No, Bunny-Runny," he said, "I can't help you. I'm very frightened myself."

So Bunny-Runny Rabbit went and sat under a tree again and he cried and cried.

All of a sudden a Wolf came stalking up.

"Why are you crying, Bunny-Runny?" asked the Wolf.

"How can I help it, Howly-Prowly, when a terrible beast is sitting in my hut!"

Said the Wolf:

"I am going to chase him out!"

"I don't believe it. The Bear tried and he couldn't, so how can you?"

"Don't worry, you can depend on me." And off the Wolf ran to the hut.

"Who, who is sitting in Bunny-Runny's hut?" he called.

And the Goat replied:

"I am Nibbly-Quibbly the Goat,
With a torn skin and coat,
To the fair I was brought
And for three groshes bought.
I will frighten you off with a bleat,
I will stamp-stamp on you with my feet,
With my horns I will hook you and crush you,
With my tail away I will brush you,
And that will be the end of you!"

The Wolf was very frightened and out he ran.

"No, Bunny-Runny," he said, "I can't help you. I am frightened myself."

And Bunny-Runny Rabbit went and sat under a tree again and he cried and cried.

All of a sudden a Fox came scampering up and she saw the Rabbit and asked:

"Why are you crying, Bunny-Runny?"

"How can I help it, Smily-Wily, when a terrible beast is sitting in my hut!"

Said the Fox:

"I am going to chase him out!"

"I don't believe it, Smily-Wily. The Bear tried and he couldn't, and the Wolf tried and he couldn't, so how can you?"

"Don't worry, you can depend on me." And off the Fox ran to the Rabbit's hut.

"Who, who is sitting in this hut?" she called. And the Goat replied:

"I am Nibbly-Quibbly the Goat,
With a torn skin and coat,
To the fair I was brought
And for three groshes bought.
I will frighten you off with a bleat,
I will stamp-stamp on you with my feet,
With my horns I will hook you and crush you,
With my tail away I will brush you,
And that will be the end of you!"

The Fox was very frightened and out she ran.

"No, Bunny-Runny," she said, "I can't help you. I am frightened myself."

And so Bunny-Runny Rabbit went and sat under a tree again and he cried and cried.

And of a sudden a Crayfish came crawling up.

"Why are you crying, Bunny-Runny?" asked the Crayfish.

40

"How can I help it when a terrible beast is sitting in my hut!"

Said the Crayfish:

"I am going to chase him out!"

"I don't believe it. The Bear tried and he couldn't, the Wolf tried and he couldn't, the Fox tried and she couldn't, so how can you?"

"Well, just see if I don't!"

And the Crayfish crawled into the Rabbit's hut and called out:

"Who, who is sitting in this hut?"

And the Goat replied:

> "I am Nibbly-Quibbly the Goat,
> With a torn skin and coat,
> To the fair I was brought
> And for three groshes bought.
> I will frighten you off with a bleat,
> I will stamp-stamp on you with my feet,
> With my horns I will hook you and crush you,
> With my tail away I will brush you,
> And that will be the end of you!"

But the Crayfish crawled on and he crawled up on the stove and hissed:

> "I'm a Crayfish, am I,   I snap—and you leap,
> And I won't pass you by.   I nip—and you weep!"

And he nipped the Goat with his claws!

The Goat gave a bleat, jumped down from the stove, ran out of the hut and was never seen again!

And Bunny-Runny Rabbit was overjoyed and he came into the hut and thanked the Crayfish over and over again. And there he lives in his hut to this day as happy as you please.

SERKO

There once lived a man who had a dog named Serko. The dog was very, very old, and one day his Master chased him out of the house. Serko went roaming through the fields, feeling quite sad and crestfallen.

"I served my Master for many years," said he to himself, "and I watched over his house, and now that I'm old and weak, he grudges me even a crust of bread and has chased me away."

Thus thought Serko when all of a sudden he saw a Wolf coming near. The Wolf approached Serko and said to him:

"What are you roaming about like that for?"

And Serko replied:

"There's nothing else I can do, for my Master has chased me away."

Said the Wolf:

"If you like, I can help you win back your Master's favour."

Serko was overjoyed.

"Do help me, my dear friend," he said. "I will find a way to repay you for your kindness."

"Well, then, listen to me," said the Wolf. "Your Master and Mistress will soon go out to the fields to do their reaping and the Mistress is sure to put her baby under a wheat stack. Now you must stay close to the baby so I'll know where he is. I'll snatch him up and carry him off and you must run after me and try to take him away. Then I'll pretend I'm frightened and let him go."

By and by the Master and Mistress went out to the fields to reap. The Mistress put her baby under a stack and herself went about her work with not a thought of danger. All of a sudden a Wolf came running up. He seized the baby and ran off with him across the field.

Serko ran after the Wolf, and Serko's Master cried in a voice that was hoarse with horror:

"Catch him, Serko!"

Serko caught up the Wolf, snatched the baby away, brought it back and placed it before his Master. And the Master took some bread and a piece of bacon out of a sack and said:

"Eat your fill, Serko! This is to thank you for saving my child!"

In the evening the Master and Mistress went home and they took Serko along with them. They entered the house and the Master said:

"Make us some *galushki*, wife, the more the better, and don't spare the lard!"

Well, when the galushki were ready, the Master seated Serko at the table and sat down beside him. Said he to his wife:

"Serve up the galushki, wife, we're going to have our supper!"

The wife set the galushki on the table and the husband laid a whole pile of them in a dish for Serko. He even blew on the galushki for fear Serko would burn himself.

And Serko sat there and he thought:

"This is all the Wolf's doing. I must repay him for his kindness whatever else I do."

Now it so happened that the Master was marrying off his eldest daughter.

Serko went out to the fields, found the Wolf there and said to him:

"Come to our vegetable garden Sunday night. I will take you into the hut and repay you for your kindness."

The Wolf waited till Sunday came round and then he went to the place Serko had named.

Now it was on that very day that the wedding was celebrated. Serko took the Wolf into the hut and hid him under the table. Then he took a bottle of vodka and a goodly piece of meat from the table and carried them to the Wolf. The guests wanted to beat the dog, but the Master would not let them and said:

"Do not touch Serko! He has done me a great service, and I shall be kind to him till the day he dies."

And Serko took some of the best pieces from the table and he carried them to the Wolf. So well did he feast him that the Wolf became quite gay and said:

"I'm going to sing!"

Now this frightened Serko very much indeed.

"Please don't," he begged, "or you will fare badly. I shall give you some more vodka if only you do me a favour and keep quiet."

The Wolf had some more vodka and then he said:

"Now I'm really going to sing!"

And he let out a terrific howl from under the table!

The guests jumped up from their seats, rushed hither and thither and tried to crawl under the table, but lo! —there was the Wolf! Some of the guests ran away in fright, and some wanted to kill the Wolf. Then Serko jumped on the Wolf's back and made as though he were about to strangle him.

Said the Master:

"Don't touch the Wolf or you might hurt Serko! And don't worry. He'll give him a sound thrashing."

And Serko took the Wolf to the field and said to him:

"You did me a kindness once and now I have paid you back."

And after that they said good-bye and went their separate ways.

TRIXY-VIXY FOX

One day Trixy-Vixy Fox felt she would like to have a bit of honey for dinner. She was tired of having only meat every day and never getting to try anything sweet.

"I think I'll go and visit the bees," she said, "and help myself to some of their delicious honey."

She came to the bee-garden, sat down very quietly in front of a hive and thrust her paw inside to scoop the honey out. Well, the bees did not like it one bit. They buzzed and they droned and they burst out of the hive, and the whole swarm of them flew at Trixy-Vixy Fox. And Trixy-Vixy Fox took to her heels and ran as fast as her legs could carry her. She ran and she ran and she twitched her nose and said:

"The honey is sweet, but the bees are bitter!"

She came home, her muzzle all swollen, and lay down to rest. She lay there a long time and she thought and thought, but she could not get the honey out of her head.

"I think I'll go to see Grumbly-Rumbly Bear," said she to herself, "and ask him to let me live in his house. He must have quite a bit of honey stored up."

And off she went to Grumbly-Rumbly Bear's house.

"Good morning, Grumbly-Rumbly," said she. "Do listen to me."

But Grumbly-Rumbly Bear only growled.

"Please, Grumbly-Rumbly, don't growl, you frighten me," begged Trixy-Vixy Fox. "Let me come and live with you and keep house."

"Very well, I'm willing," said Grumbly-Rumbly Bear.

And so the two of them began to keep house together. Grumbly-Rumbly Bear would go out hunting and he would bring enough meat for both himself and Trixy-Vixy Fox. But Trixy-Vixy Fox still wanted honey more than anything.

"Do go to the bee-garden, Grumbly-Rumbly," she begged, "and get me some honey. I'm dying to have something sweet!"

And off Grumbly-Rumbly Bear went and he brought back two whole hives full of honey.

"Here you are," he said. "We'll eat up one of these, and we'll store the other up for the winter."

So they ate the honey and ate the honey and after a time the first of the hives was empty. And they hid the second hive away in the attic.

Grumbly-Rumbly Bear was patient, but Trixy-Vixy Fox kept thinking about the honey and wondering how to get at it. She could not very well climb up to the attic, for Grumbly-Rumbly Bear would then ask her what she wanted there. So she lay on her bed and she went knock-knock against the wall with her tail.

"Who is that knocking?" asked Grumbly-Rumbly Bear.

"That's the neighbours calling me. A son was born to them."

"Well, go along, and I'll stay here and sleep."

So off went Trixy-Vixy Fox, and she climbed up to the attic and had her fill of the honey. She came back after a while, and Grumbly-Rumbly Bear said to her:

"What name did they give the little boy?"

"Top-Licked-Off," said Trixy-Vixy Fox.

"What an odd name!"

"What's odd about it? Tastes differ!"

"Oh, never mind!"

On the next day Trixy-Vixy Fox lay on her bed again and she went knock-knock against the wall with her tail.

"Who is that knocking?" asked Grumbly-Rumbly Bear.

"That's the neighbours calling me. A daughter was born to them."

"Well, go along, and I'll stay here and sleep."

Trixy-Vixy Fox ran to the attic and she helped herself to such a generous portion of the honey that hardly anything was left in the hive.

She came back to the hut and Grumbly-Rumbly Bear woke up and asked:

"Well, what name did they give the little girl?"

"Less-And-Waning," replied Trixy-Vixy Fox.

"What an odd name!"

"Not at all! I think it's a nice name."

"Oh, have it your way!"

On the third day Trixy-Vixy Fox again went knock-knock against the wall with her tail.

"Someone's knocking again," said Grumbly-Rumbly Bear.

"That's the neighbours. Another son was born to them."

"Why do they keep calling you so often?"

"They like my company, that's why."

"Well, go along!"

So off Trixy-Vixy Fox ran to the attic. She ate up all the honey, turned the hive over and licked off the walls! Then she came back to the hut and curled up on her bed again.

"What name did they give this little boy?" asked Grumbly-Rumbly Bear.

"A very simple one," Trixy-Vixy Fox replied, "All-Scraped-Out."

"What! Who has ever heard of such a name?"

"What do you know about it! There must be such a name if they've given it to the boy."

"Anything is possible," said Grumbly-Rumbly Bear. But after a time he said to himself:

"I think I'd like to have a bit of honey!"

He climbed up to the attic and looked in and there was the hive—quite empty!

"It was you who ate the honey, Trixy-Vixy!" cried Grumbly-Rumbly Bear. "Now I'm going to eat you up!"

And he ran after Trixy-Vixy Fox. But Trixy-Vixy Fox was **too** quick for him. She **ran** off to the forest and that was the last he ever saw of her!

THE POLECAT

Once upon a time there lived an Old Man and an Old Woman. Now it so happened that a Polecat fell into the habit of coming to their house and of stealing their chickens. He stole all the young chicks and then he came and carried away the mother-hen.

Said the Old Man:

"I think I'll go and give the Polecat a beating."
And off he went.

He walked and he walked and he saw a pumpkin-peel lying on the road.

"Where are you going, Grandpa?" asked the Pumpkin-Peel.

"To give the Polecat a beating," the Old Man replied.

"May I come with you?"

"Come along."

So the two of them went on together, and they saw some bast lying on the road.

"Where are you going, Grandpa?" asked the Bast.

"To give the Polecat a beating."

"May I come with you?"

"Come along."

So the three of them went on together and they saw a stick lying on the road.

"Where are you going, Grandpa?" asked the Stick.

"To give the Polecat a beating."

"May I come with you?"

"Come along."

So the four of them went on together and they saw an acorn lying on the road.

"Where are you going, Grandpa?" asked the Acorn.

"To give the Polecat a beating."

"May I come with you?"

"Come along."

So the five of them went on together and they saw a crayfish crawling along.

"Where are you going, Grandpa?" asked the Crayfish.

"To give the Polecat a beating."

"May I come with you?"

"Come along."

So the six of them went on together and they saw a cock running toward them.

"Where are you going, Grandpa?" asked the Cock.

"To give the Polecat a beating."

"May I come with you?"

"Come along."

So the seven of them went on together and they came to the Polecat's hut. They looked in through the window, but the Polecat was nowhere to be seen. So they came into the hut and hid there. The Acorn climbed into the stove, the Pumpkin-Peel lay down on the doorstep and the Bast just under, the Stick got up on the berth, the Crayfish jumped into a tub, the Cock flew up on a perch and the Old Man climbed up on the stove.

By and by the Polecat ran in and the Acorn in the stove, all hot and steaming, sang out:

"Polecat, Polecat, hear my say,
You have visitors today.
Polecat, Polecat, be on guard,
We will thrash you very hard.
And, before I count to ten,
Free the chickens and the hen."

"What, what was that?" the Polecat cried.

But the Acorn went on singing, and it was so hot in the stove that by and by there came from it nothing but a crack-crack and a p-ff-t!

The Polecat was very frightened and he rushed to the tub, but the Crayfish nipped him in the leg. He tried to climb up on the perch, but the Cock pecked him in the head. He ran to the doorstep, but he slipped on the Pumpkin-Peel. He fell and he was tangled up in the Bast. Then the Stick jumped down from the berth and began to thrash him very hard—whack! whack!

And as for the Old Man, he took the mother-hen and the baby chicks and went his way in peace.

THE GOAT AND THE RAM

There once lived an Old Man and an Old Woman who had a Goat and a Ram. The Goat and the Ram were great friends: wherever the Goat went, there the Ram was sure to go, too. The Goat would go to the vegetable garden to get some cabbage, and the Ram did the same; the Goat would go to the orchard, and there was the Ram on his heels.

"Old Woman," said the Old Man, "let us chase away the Goat and the Ram, for there's no keeping them out of our orchard and kitchen garden. Go away, you two, and never let me see you again!"

So the Goat and the Ram made themselves a sack and off they went. They walked and they walked and suddenly they saw a wolf's head lying in the middle of a field. Now the Ram was very strong, but not very brave, and the Goat was very brave, but not very strong.

Said the Goat:

"Take the wolf's head, Ram, for you are the stronger."

"Oh, no, Goat, you take it, for you are the braver."

Then they took hold of the wolf's head together, stuffed it into the sack and went their way further.

They walked and they walked and by and by they saw a light burning just ahead.

"That must be a house," said they. "Let us go and spend the night there. The Wolves will never get us if we do."

They went toward the light, and lo and behold! It came from a fire over which several Wolves were cooking porridge.

"Hello there, friends!" called the Goat and the Ram.

"Hello!" the Wolves called back. "It's a good thing you've come. While our porridge is cooking, we shall feast on your flesh."

At this the Goat was much alarmed, and the Ram nearly died of fright.

Said the Goat:

"Take the wolf's head out of the sack, Brother Ram!"

The Ram did as he was told, and the Goat said:

"Not that one. The bigger one!"

The Ram started taking out the very same head, and the Goat said again:

"No! Take out the biggest one!"

Now this startled the Wolves very much indeed and they began to think of a way of making their escape. For there was the Ram taking one wolf's head after another out of the sack!

Said one of the Wolves:

"We're a nice, friendly company gathered here, brothers, and the porridge is cooking well. All it needs is a little more water. I think I'll go and fetch some."

He walked a short way off and said, but so that they could not hear, "A plague on you and your company!" And then he took to his heels.

Now the second Wolf began to think and to wonder how he could best make his escape.

"Look at that rascal!" said he about the first Wolf. "It's as though the earth had swallowed him! He's never brought the water for the porridge. I think I'll take a switch and go bring him back."

And off he went and never came back, either.

And the third Wolf sat there for a while and he said:

"I think I'll go and bring the two of them back!"

And off he ran and was very glad to have had such a narrow escape.

Said the Goat to the Ram:

"Quick, Brother Ram, there's no time to be wasted. Let us eat the porridge and run for our lives."

Meanwhile the first Wolf thought and thought and then he said:

"Whatever made us fear the Goat and Ram, brothers? Let us go back and eat them up, the rascals!"

The Wolves went back, but by that time the Goat and the Ram had finished their porridge, put out the fire and climbed up a tall oak-tree. There they sat, and the Wolves never saw them. They stood under the tree and they thought and wondered how best to overtake the Goat and the Ram. And after a while they looked up, and there were the Goat and the Ram on the oak-tree. The Goat, who was the braver of the two, had climbed to the very top of the tree, and the Ram, who was not so brave, was sitting a little lower.

"Well," said the Wolves to the shaggiest one among them, "you are the eldest, so you must tell us how to make them come down."

The Shaggy Wolf lay down under the tree and began to think and to wonder what he should do.

As for the Ram, he was sitting on his branch and trembling. He tr-r-r-embled and tr-r-r-embled and he lost his balance and tumbled down, straight on top of the Shaggy Wolf. And the Goat didn't think long before he cried:

"Hand me over that shaggy one!"

And he came down straight on top of the Wolves.

The Wolves started up and they took to their heels down the road, raising clouds of dust as they ran.

And the Goat and the Ram built themselves a little hut and they lived there in health and cheer and grew richer from year to year.

SMILY-WILY THE FOX

One day Smily-Wily the Fox stole a chicken and ran off with it down the road. She ran and she ran and after a time night drew on and it was very dark.

Smily-Wily saw a hut just ahead and she came inside, bowed low to the people who lived there and said:

"Good evening, good people!"

"Good evening to you, Smily-Wily!"

"Do let me pass the night in your hut!"

"But, Smily-Wily, we haven't got any room, there's no place to put you."

"Never mind! Under that bench will I make my bed, with my bushy tail over my head, and that's how I'll spend the night."

"Very well, you can stay!"

"Where shall I put my chicken?"

"Under the stove."

Smily-Wily did as she was told, but when night came she got up very quietly, ate up the chicken and whisked all the feathers away into a corner. And in the morning, she rose very early, washed herself very white, wished her hosts a good morning and said:

"Where's my chicken?"

"Under the stove."

"I looked, but it wasn't there." And she sat down and began to weep.

"My chicken was all I had in the world, and even that was stolen from me. You must give me a duck in return."

And nothing would do but they must give her the duck. And Smily-Wily took the duck, put it in her sack and went on her way.

She ran and she ran and night drew on and she was still on the road. She saw a hut standing there and she came inside and said:

"Good evening, good people!"

"Good evening to you, Smily-Wily!"

"Let me pass the night in your hut."

"Our hut is so small, there's no place to put you."

"Never mind! Under that bench will I make my bed, with my bushy tail over my head, and that's how I'll spend the night."

"Very well, you can stay!"

"Where shall I put my duck?"

"In the goose-pen."

Smily-Wily did as she was told, but when night came, she got up very quietly, ate up the duck and raked the feathers into a heap. And in the morning, she rose very early, washed herself very white, wished her hosts a good morning and said:

"Where is my duck?"

They looked into the goose-pen, but the duck was not there. Said the master of the house:

"Perhaps we've let it out with the geese?"

And Smily-Wily burst out weeping.

"The duck was all I had in the world, and even that is gone!" she cried. "You must give me a goose in return!"

And nothing would do but they must give her the goose.

And Smily-Wily took the goose, put it in her sack and went on her way.

She walked and she walked till night drew on again. She saw a hut, came inside and said:

"Good evening, good people! Do let me pass the night in your hut!"

"We can't do that, Smily-Wily, we haven't got any room!"

"Never mind! Under that bench will I make my bed, with my bushy tail over my head, and that's how I'll spend the night."

"Very well, you can stay!"

"Where shall I put my goose?"

"In the barn with the ewe-lambs."

Smily-Wily did as she was told, but when night came, she got up very quietly, ate up the goose and raked the feathers into a heap. And in the morning, she rose very early, washed very white, wished her hosts a good morning and asked:

"Where is my goose?"

They went and looked, but the goose was gone.

Said Smily-Wily:

"Such a thing has never happened to me before, no matter where I was or spent the night. Nothing was ever lost."

Said the master of the house:

"Maybe the ewe-lambs have trampled your goose to death?"

And Smily-Wily replied:

"That's all very well, but you must give me a lamb in return."

And nothing would do but they must give her the lamb. And Smily-Wily popped the lamb into her sack and went on her way.

She ran and she ran and, before she knew it, night fell. She saw a hut and asked to be let in for the night.

"Do let me in, good people!" she begged.

"We can't do that, Smily-Wily, we haven't got any room. There's no place to put you."

"Never mind! Under a bench will I make my bed, with my bushy tail over my head, and that's how I'll spend the night."

"Very well, you can stay!"

"Where shall I put my lamb?"

"Leave it in the yard."

Smily-Wily did as she was told, but when night came, she got up very quietly and ate up the lamb. And in the morning, she rose very early and washed very white and said just as she had so many times before:

"Where is my lamb?"

And she sat down and wept and wept.

"Such a thing has never happened to me before, no matter where I was or spent the night."

Said the master of the house:

"Perhaps my daughter-in-law let it out as she drove the bullocks to water?"

Said Smily-Wily:

"That is all very well, but you must give me your daughter-in-law in return for my lamb."

The old man cried and the old woman cried and their son cried and their son's children cried, but Smily-Wily seized the old man's daughter-in-law and whisked her into her sack. She tied the sack with a rope and then she left the hut for a few moments. And the old man's son let his wife out of the sack and put a dog in instead.

Smily-Wily came back and she took up the sack and carried it off with her. She walked and she walked and she said:

"A duck for the chicken, a goose for the duck, a lamb for the goose and a young wife for the lamb!"

She shook the sack and the dog inside it went: "G-r-r!"

Said Smily-Wily:

"The old man's daughter-in-law is so frightened, she howls! I think I'll peep inside and take a look at her."

She undid the sack and lo! out the dog jumped with a bow-wow-wow!

Smily-Wily bolted away, and the dog ran after her. Smily-Wily ran deeper and deeper into the forest, and there was the dog on her heels! But at last Smily-Wily ran up to her fox-hole and hid there. She sat in the hole, and the dog stood over it and couldn't get in.

Said Smily-Wily:

"Little Ears, Little Ears!
Come, tell me why, on this fine day
From that meany-mean dog you ran away?"

And the Little Ears replied:

"'Twas, Smily-Wily, that we feared to behold
That meany-mean dog tear your coat of gold!"

"Thank you, Little Ears, I shall buy you a pair of gold earrings for this," said Smily-Wily, and she called out again:

"Little Feet, Little Feet!
Come, tell me why, on this fine day
From that meany-mean dog you ran away?"

And the Little Feet replied:

> "'Twas, Smily-Wily, that we feared to behold
> That meany-mean dog tear your coat of gold.
> And we went not slow, we went quick as quick,
> We ran ahead with a blickerty-blick!"

"Thank you, Little Feet, thank you kindly. I shall buy you a pair of gold boots with silver heels," said Smily-Wily, and she called again:

> "Little Big Tail, broom-brush-stick,
> What made you rush away so quick
> From that meany-mean dog on this bright day?
> Little Big Tail, come tell me, pray!"

And the Little Big Tail replied:

> "I went off in a rush, but I caught in the brush,
> And I whipped you,
> And I tripped you,
> And I went slow as slow, I went not fast,
> For I wanted to see you caught at last!"

Smily-Wily was very angry and she stuck her tail out of the burrow and said:

"If that is so, then, dog, you may have my tail. Bite off as much of it as you can!"

And the dog sank his teeth into the tail so hard that he bit off the whole of it!

After a while Smily-Wily thought she would like to pay the rabbits a visit, and off she went.

When the rabbits saw that she was tailless, they nearly split their sides laughing.

Said Smily-Wily:

"I may not have a tail, but I can lead a ring dance better than any of you."

"How do you go about it?"

"That's simple. I have only to tie your tails together, and you'll learn at once."

"Well, go ahead."

So Smily-Wily tied all the rabbits together by their tails and herself sprang up on a mound and shouted at the top of her voice:

"Run for your lives! Big Teeth the Wolf is coming!"

And the rabbits tried to run and they pulled and struggled and their tails came straight off!

Then they put their heads together and began to think of a way to repay Smily-Wily for what she did. But Smily-Wily heard them and she knew she would fare badly. So off she ran from the forest as fast as her legs would carry her. And that was the last that ever was seen of her.

As for the rabbits, they have gone without their tails ever since.

THE POOR WOLF

Once upon a time there lived a poor Wolf who nearly died of hunger because he could not find any food for himself. So off he went to a Peasant's house to ask for something to eat. And he pretended to be very, very poor indeed!

"Do have pity on me, Peasant," he said. "Give me something to eat or I shall die of hunger."

"What would you like?" the Peasant asked.

"Anything will do," the Wolf replied.

"Well, do you see the priest's mare grazing in the meadow there? Why don't you go and eat her? She's easy enough to catch."

So off the Wolf ran—clumpety-clump!—to the meadow.

"Good morning, Mare!" he called. "The Peasant has told me to eat you."

"Who are you that you want to eat me?" asked the Mare.

"I'm a Wolf."

"You're lying, you're only a Dog!"

"No, I'm a Wolf, I swear it!"

"Well, if that is so, which part of me will you begin on first?"

"Your head!" said the Wolf.

"My head?" said the Mare. "You poor, poor Wolf! If you really intend to eat me, you had better begin with my tail. While you are eating your way to my middle, I'll still be grazing, and I'll be nice and fat by the time you are ready to eat the rest of me."

"Very well, that sounds reasonable!" said the Wolf, and he made a lunge for the Mare's tail. He seized the tail with his teeth, but the Mare kicked out and struck him with her hoof across his muzzle so hard that the Wolf did not know if he was dead or alive. And the Mare galloped off, raising clouds of dust as she ran.

The Wolf sat there and he thought:

"Fool that I am! Why didn't I seize her by the throat?" And back he went to the Peasant's house to ask for food again.

"Please, Peasant," he said, "have pity on me! Give me something to eat, if only a morsel, or I shall die of hunger."

"Wasn't the mare enough for you?" asked the Peasant.

At that the Wolf let out a great howl.

"The mare!" he cried. "I hope they skin her alive and make leather straps out of her! Why, she squashed my whole muzzle for me!"

"Well, if that is so," said the Peasant, "then go and eat that fat ram over there, grazing on the hilltop."

So off the Wolf ran, and, sure enough, there was the Ram.

"Hello, Ram!" said the Wolf.

"Hello!"

"The Peasant has told me to eat you."

"And who are you that you want to eat me?"

"A Wolf."

"You're lying, you're a Dog!"

"No, I'm a Wolf, I swear it!"

"Well, if that is so, how will you go about eating me?"

"That's simple! I'll begin with your head."

"My head!" said the Ram. "Ah, you poor, poor Wolf! If you really intend to eat me, you must stand on the hill-top and open your mouth wide and I'll jump straight in."

So the Wolf went and stood on the hill-top and he opened his jaws so wide that you could see right down into his maw. And the Ram ran straight at him and he struck the Wolf in the head with his horns and sent him rolling down the hill-side. A fine mouthful did the Wolf get!

He sat up then, the poor thing, and began to cry.

"Fool that I am!" he said. "Where were my wits? Who has ever heard of food jumping into one's mouth of itself?"

He thought and he thought and after a while he went back to the Peasant's house to ask for food again.

"Please, Peasant," he said, "have pity on me! Give me something to eat or I shall die of hunger."

Said the Peasant:

"A fine eater you are, I must say! You want food to jump into your mouth of itself. But what's the use of trying to make you see reason? An Old Woman has lost a piece of bacon on the road there. Go and eat it. The bacon will surely be yours, it can't run away."

And the Wolf did as the Peasant told him to. He went down the road and found the bacon. He sat down in front of it and he said to himself:

"This is all very well, but the bacon must be salty and is sure to make me very thirsty. I had better go and have a drink of water first."

So off he went to the river.

In the meantime the Old Woman missed her bacon and went back in search of it. And lo! there it lay on the road. So she picked it up and went on her way.

After a while the Wolf came back, but the bacon was gone. The Wolf sat down on the road and he began to cry.

"Fool that I am!" he said. "Where were my wits? Who has ever heard of anyone drinking before he eats?"

He sat there a long time thinking and, oh! how ter-r-r-ibly hungry he became.

So he went again to the Peasant's house to ask for food.

"Please, Peasant," he said, "have pity on me! Give me something to eat or it'll be the end of me."

"You make me sick with your begging," said the Peasant, "but what's to be done with the likes of you! There's a pig grazing near the village. Go and eat her."

So off the Wolf went and he soon saw the Pig.

"Hello, Pig!" he said. "The Peasant has told me to eat you."

"Who are you that you want to eat me?" asked the Pig.

"I'm a Wolf."

"You're lying, you're a Dog."

"No, I'm a Wolf!"

"And can't wolves get any food for themselves now-adays?"

"No, they can't."

"If that is so, then get on my back, and I will take you to the village. They are choosing the elders there today, so, perhaps, they'll choose you!"

"Very well, let's go!"

So the Wolf climbed up on the Pig's back and off they ran. They came to the village, and the Pig began to grunt so loudly that the Wolf was quite frightened.

"What are you grunting like that for?" he asked.

And the Pig said:

"I'm calling the villagers together so that they can choose you their elder."

And, sure enough, the villagers soon came running up with pokers, prongs and shovels, whatever they had been able to get their hands on. The sight of them took the Wolf's breath away, he was so startled.

"Why are so many people running here?" asked he of the Pig in a whisper.

"To see you," the Pig replied.

And lo! the villagers surrounded the Wolf and began to beat and to thrash him so hard that he quite forgot his hunger. He rushed headlong down the road and ran straight into a tailor who was coming along that way with his yardstick in his hand.

"I am going to eat you up," the Wolf said.

"Who are you that you think of doing such a thing?"

"I'm a Wolf."

"You're lying, you're a Dog."

"No, I'm a Wolf, I swear it!"

"You look small for a Wolf. Here, let me measure you."

And the Tailor twisted the Wolf's tail round and round his hand and began to beat him with his stick, saying:

"One yard in length, one yard in breadth!"

And the Wolf was so frightened that off he ran as fast as his legs could carry him! This time, however, he didn't go to see the Peasant but his own brothers the Wolves.

"Little Brothers!" he cried. "Something terrible has happened to me!"

He told them the whole story, and the Wolves set off at a run after the Tailor!

Here was a fine kettle of fish! What was the Tailor to do? He looked all around, and he saw a tree. So up he climbed to its very top, and the Wolves stood round the tree and gnashed their teeth.

Said the Poor Wolf:

"No, Little Brothers, we shall never get him this way. Here is what we must do. I shall stand on the ground and one of you will stand on my back and someone else on his and so on till we have a real ladder!"

And the Wolves did as the Poor Wolf told them and climbed up on one another's backs.

The one on the very top said:

"Well, Tailor, you had better climb down. We are going to eat you up."

"Oh," said the Tailor, "do have pity on me, Little Brothers, please don't eat me!"

"But we must," said the Wolves, "so don't waste time!"

"Wait," said the Tailor again, "you might at least let me take a sniff of my tobacco before I die."

He sniffed his tobacco and—ap-che!—let out a great sneeze!

And the Poor Wolf who was at the bottom of the ladder thought that the Tailor was beating the top

Wolf and saying "a yard in length" and he crouched down in fright, sending the rest of the Wolves rolling to the ground in a heap! The Poor Wolf took to his heels and the rest of the Wolves followed. And the Tailor climbed down from the tree and went his way home.

And there he lives with his wife, and they
Feast on tarts and dumplings all the day!
I was there and I ate and drank until
Of the mead and the wine I had my fill.
But if someone asks, I won't deny
That my beard was wet, but my mouth was dry!

So here for me is a keg of ale,
And for you, a nice long tale;
And there for me is a jug of honey,
And for you, a bag of money.

LITTLE SISTER FOX
AND LITTLE BROTHER WOLF

Once upon a time there was a Fox who thought it would be very nice to have a hut. So she built herself one and she lived there very snugly indeed.

Then winter came, and the Fox was very cold. So off she ran to the village to fetch a light for her stove. She came to an Old Woman's house and said:

"Good morning, Old Woman! I hope you are well. Do give me a light, and I shall do as much for you some day."

"Very well, Little Sister, sit down and warm up while I take my baking out of the stove."

Now the Old Woman was baking some poppy-seed cakes. She took them out of the stove and put them on the table to cool. And the Fox looked and she snatched up a cake that was bigger and browner than the rest and made off with it as fast as ever she could. She ate up all of the poppy-seed filling, stuffed the cake full of sweepings and dust, covered them over with the crust and set off at a run again.

She ran and she ran till she saw two shepherd boys driving a herd of cows to water.

Said the Fox:

"Good morning, my fine lads!"

"Good morning to you, Little Sister!"

"Let's trade! You give me a yearling bull and I'll give you this poppy-seed cake."

"Very well."

"But you mustn't eat the cake till I leave the village."

So the Fox gave the shepherds the cake in return for a yearling bull. She made off with the Bull for the forest, and the shepherds began to eat the cake and found it stuffed with sweepings and dust.

And Little Sister the Fox came to her hut and she cut down a tree and made herself a sledge. She harnessed the Little Bull to the sledge and went driving along, and lo and behold!--a Wolf came running up.

"Good morning, Little Sister!" he called.

"Good morning to you, Little Brother!"

"Where did you get the Bull and the sledge?"

"I made them!"

Said the Wolf:

"Do let me ride with you a little way!"

"How can I do that? You'll break the sledge."

"No, I won't. I'll just put one of my legs on it."

"Oh, very well."

So the Fox and the Wolf went driving along together, and by and by the Wolf said:

"I think I'll put my second leg on the sledge, Little Sister."

"Oh, but you'll break the sledge, Little Brother."

"No, I won't."

"Well, go ahead, then."

So the Wolf put his second leg on the sledge and he and the Fox went driving along when suddenly there came a c-r-rack!

"Stop, Little Brother, you're breaking my sledge!" cried the Fox.

"No, Little Sister, I was just cracking a nut."

"Oh, well, if that was all!"

So the two of them went driving along again, and by and by the Wolf said:

"Little Sister, I think I'll put my third leg on the sledge."

"Don't be silly! You'll break it, and then what'll I have to carry my wood on?"

"Don't be afraid, I won't."

"Oh, very well, then."

So the Wolf put his third leg on the sledge and something went c-r-r-r-ack!—again.

"Dear me!" said the Fox. "You'd better go away, Little Brother, or you'll break my sledge all up!"

"No, Little Sister, I was just cracking a nut."

"Give me one!"

"I haven't any more. That was the last."

So they went driving along again, and by and by the Wolf said:

"I think I'll climb into your sledge, all of me now, Little Sister!"

"You mustn't do that, Little Brother, you'll break the sledge!"

"No, I won't. I'll be careful."

"Well, see that you are!"

So the Wolf climbed into the sledge, and, of course, he broke it all up. And the Fox began to scold him. She scolded him and she scolded him and then she said:

"Go and cut down a tree, you bad so-and-so, chop it up into logs, put the logs on the sledge and bring them here."

"How will I do that?" said the Wolf. "I don't know which tree you want."

"You bad so-and-so, you knew very well how to break my sledge, but when I want a tree cut, you pretend you don't know how."

And she began to scold him again. She scolded him and she scolded him and then she said:

"As soon as you come to the forest, you must say: 'Tree, tree, straight and crooked, cut yourself up into logs! Tree, tree, straight and crooked, cut yourself up into logs!'"

So off the Wolf went.

He came to the forest and he said:

"Tree, tree, crooked and crooked, cut yourself up into logs! Tree, tree, crooked and crooked, cut yourself up into logs!"

And the tree did as it was told. The logs were so twisted and knobby that not even a stick could be made out of them, to say nothing of sledge runners.

The Wolf took the logs to the Fox, and the Fox threw one look at them and began to scold the Wolf harder than ever.

"You bad so-and-so," she said, "you must have said the wrong words!"

"Well, Little Sister, I stood there and said: 'Tree, tree, crooked and crooked, cut yourself up into logs!'"

"I knew it! What a blunderhead you are! Sit here, and I'll go and cut the wood myself."

And off the Fox went.

There sat the Wolf and by and by he began to grow very hungry. He looked all over the Fox's hut, but found nothing. He thought and he thought and he said to himself:

"I think I'll eat the Little Bull and run away."

He made a little hole in the Little Bull's side, ate up what was inside, stuffed it full with sparrows, closed the hole up with a handful of straw and himself ran off as fast as his legs could carry him.

By and by the Fox came back from the forest. She made herself a new sledge, climbed in and said:

"Giddy-up, Little Bull!"

But never a move did the Little Bull make.

Then the Fox took up a stick and she gave the Little Bull such a blow that the handful of straw fell from his side and the sparrows flew out with a wh-i-r-r!

"You wicked thing!" cried the Fox. (She meant the Wolf, you see.) "You wait, I'll pay you back for this!"

And off she went.

She stretched herself out on the road and lay there very quietly.

By and by some Ox-Drivers came driving up with a train of fish. And the Fox lay without stirring and pretended to be dead.

The Ox-Drivers saw her and said:

"Let's take the Fox, brothers, and sell her."

So they threw the Fox on the last cart and drove on. They drove and they drove, and the Fox saw that they never looked back and began to throw the fish down from the cart. She threw one fish down after another and when there were quite a few on the road, she quietly climbed down herself. The Ox-Drivers drove on, and the Fox gathered up the fish into a pile, sat down and began to eat.

By and by the Wolf came running up.

"Hello there, Little Sister!" he called.

"Hello yourself, Little Brother!"

"What are you doing, Little Sister?"

"Eating fish."

"Give me some!"

"Go and catch some for yourself."

"How can I do that? I don't know how!"

"Well, just as you like. You won't get a bone from me!"

"Won't you at least tell me how I am to go about catching it?"

And the Fox said to herself:

"You wait, Little Brother! You ate up my Little Bull, and now I'll pay you back for it!"

Then she turned to the Wolf and said:

"Go to the river, dip your tail into an ice-hole, move it slowly back and forth and say: 'Come and be caught, little fishes and big, come and be caught, little fishes and big!' That way you'll catch all the fish you want."

"Thank you for telling me," said the Wolf.

He ran to the river, dipped his tail into an ice-hole, moved it slowly back and forth and said:

"Come and be caught, little fishes and big!"

And the Fox looked out at him through the reeds on the bank and said:

"Freeze, freeze, Wolf's tail!"

Now there was a crackling frost out, and the Wolf kept moving his tail back and forth and saying:

"Come and be caught, little fishes and big!"

And the Fox kept repeating:

"Freeze, freeze, Wolf's tail!"

The Wolf stayed there catching fish till his tail was frozen fast to the ice. Then the Fox ran to the village and cried:

"Come, good people, and kill the Wolf!"

And the villagers ran to the river with pokers, prongs and axes. They fell on the Wolf and they killed him.

And as for the Fox, she still lives in her hut as snug as you please.

9 781410 107060